Bonus Books, Inc.
and
Now Comics, Inc.

THE GREEN HORNET Special Hard Bound Collector's Edition is published by Bonus Books and Now Comics (A division of Caputo Publishing, Inc.). THE GREEN HORNET is TM and © 1980, 1990 THE GREEN HORNET, INC. All other material is © 1990 Bonus Books, Inc. and Now Comics. The twelve stories are reprinted from the monthly comic published by Now Comics. THE GREEN HORNET is represented by Leisure Concepts, Inc., New York, NY. All rights reserved.

Except for appropriate use in critical reviews or works of scholarship, the reproduction or use of this work in any form or by any electronic, mechanical or other means now known or hereafter invented, including photocopying and recording, and in any information storage and retrieval system is forbidden without the written permission of the publisher.

94 93 92 91 90   5 4 3 2 1

Library of Congress Catalog Card Number: 90-82743

International Standard Book Number: 0-929387-46-5

Bonus Books, Inc.
160 East Illinois Street
Chicago, Illinois 60611

Printed in the United States of America

CONTENTS

Introduction

ISSUE

1 My Last Case

2 My Last Case—Continued

3 Legend

4 Obituaries

5 Requiem and Rebirth

6 The New Green Hornet

CONTENTS

ISSUE

7 Bloodlines

8 On the Pad

9 On the Pad—Part Two

10 The Road Pirates

11 A Memory of Death

12 A Memory of Death—Part Two

INTRODUCTION

Hello out there, Green Hornet fans. Many of you might not realize that I was just as much a Green Hornet fan as a lot of you were and are.

I followed the ''Lone Ranger and Tonto'' for many years on radio and TV, and also the old radio ''Green Hornet.'' Many an evening was spent around the radio listening to the exciting tales of ''The Green Hornet and Kato.'' I didn't really discover that the Green Hornet was a modernization of the Lone Ranger until I was signed to play the Green Hornet in the television version of the show. I thought the writers did an excellent job of adapting the shows from the old West to a modern city.

Working with Bruce Lee was a real kick. He had tremendous enthusiasm for his role as Kato, not so much for acting, but in his dedication to showcasing what he called ''Jeet Kune Do.'' This was his own in-

INTRODUCTION

terpretation of an ancient Chinese martial art learned under the tutelage of many Chinese grand masters.

Bruce's dedication to the ancient masters and his desire to follow the design they taught never wavered. He was very upset with many of the portrayals of "Kung Fu" and "Karate" that came after him and were obviously poor copies of his art.

Bruce would drive the people on the set nuts by constantly practicing his kicks and backhands on everyone. He was a perfectionist, and never wanted to portray his art in a phony way.

The people on the show, the cast, were all very friendly and worked very hard to make the show a success.

NOW Comics has come up with a very interesting concept in that they are working with three generations of Green Hornets. By developing three separate time frames to work out stories in, they have three distinct eras of history to surround their heroes with.

When I was doing the TV show, I was very insistent that we follow the original premise of the "Green Hornet," and I think we did stick to the original as close as we could, making the show very believeable. We developed many sincere fans over the years; the comic books and books are staying with the original premise and will not only keep our loyal fans, but hopefully develop new ones.

I hope to see many of you at the comic conventions and personal appearances I have lined up. I always enjoy meeting fellow fans and discussing the show or the comics, and answering any questions you may have.

Sincerely,
Van Williams

MY LAST CASE

MEMOIRS CONTINUED...

My grandfather, Dan Reid, was a Texas Ranger, as was his younger brother. When He was murdered by outlaws...

Grandmother Reid returned east and Dad completed his education at the Striker School of Journalism.

After many years of dedication to his craft, Dan Reid Jr. founded the city's first daily tabloid, THE SENTINEL, just two months after marrying Margaret Sanford.

I was born Britt Elijah Reid in 1906, two years after my brother, Jack. It was a prosperous time for the Reids.

I was practically raised with ink in my veins, and all I ever desired was to, one day, be a newshound like my old man.

Jack went on to become an architect and marry Helen Sawyer, only because he saw her first. I was best man. It was 1934, and I had just joined the Sentinel as a crime reporter.

The following year, I accompanied my parents on a two month vacation to the far east. Dad said it would broaden my horizons.

Thus, I was destined to be near at hand when a Japanese lad, named Ikano Kato, nearly drowned in Tokyo harbor by a freakish mishap.

Through some eastern code of conduct, Ikano believed himself morally indebted to me. Try as I might to persuade him, he adamantly persisted to my embarrassment.

Little did I realize, he would become my dearest and most trusted companion in a life of nerve wracking adventures.

Prohibition had been a catalyst in America, in that it contributed to the organizing of the criminal element in major cities throughout the land.

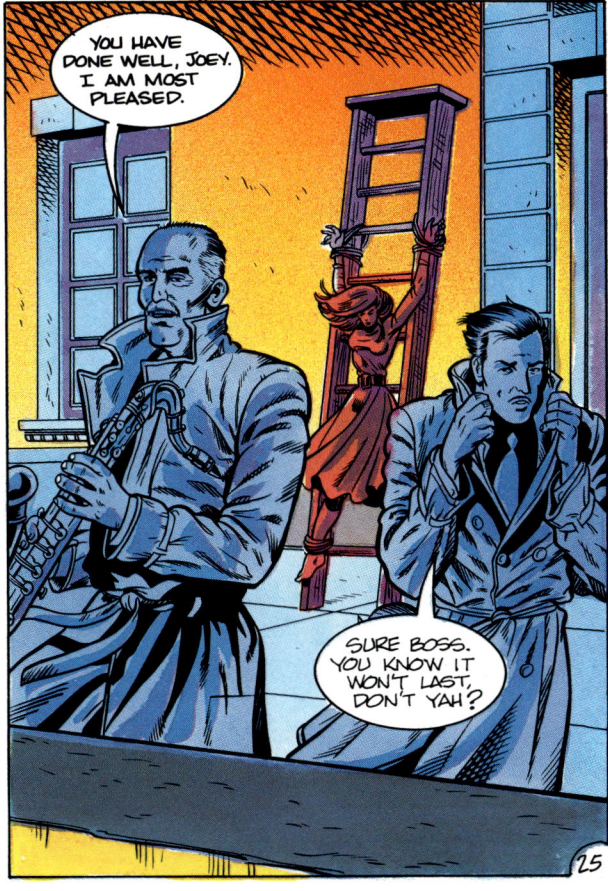

"OH, BRITT... I THOUGHT YOU WERE GOING TO DIE."

"IT'S OVER NOW... ALL OF IT."

AND SO ENDED THE LIFE OF GANG BOSS GATLAND TOBIAS AND WITH HIM THE CAREER OF THE GREEN HORNET.

MEMOIRS CONTINUED...

The destruction brought about by Gatland Tobias' insanity would make itself felt for years to come. For all of us involved, it was a time of grief and rededication.

As reports on the conditions of Hiroshima and Nagasaki continued to come in from overseas wires, all of us wondered if this new Atomic Age was in fact the final opening of Pandora's Box of doom. Dad and I worked diligently with Washington and finally managed to obtain a travel visa for Ikano. Both Ruth and I decided to advance our wedding date so that my good friend, and long time ally, could serve as my best man.

Thus, on December 8th, 1945, Ruth Andrea Hopkins became Mrs. Britt Reid. By far the wisest act of my entire life. Two days later Ikano Kato boarded a plane for Japan. Times were so hectic, there was no thought of a honeymoon, nor was I able to dwell on Ikano's departure. The Reids spent the next six months repairing and refurbishing the SENTINEL. Meanwhile, my close friend Commissioner Higgins, a true hero of what became known as Blood Wednesday, campaigned and won the post of Mayor. The Sentinel was honored to support his candidacy.

As for the survivors of Tobias' mob, most were convicted and sentenced to various terms in the state penitentiary. Foremost among these was Leo Devane. We little realized that he would be back on the streets within five years for what his parole board termed "good behavior." It should come as no surprise that he quickly regained control of the City's criminal element. He had studied under a master.

Those years were more than work and sweat; Ikano met and married a lovely maiden named Oshi Yoshura. Together they began NIPPON TOMORROW, a prospering electronics company. But I am jumping ahead of events. On March 9th, 1947, Ruth gave birth to Diana Marie Reid, who was to be our only child. She was a dark eyed copy of her mother in every way and the jewel of our lives. The following year, Ikano's first of three sons was born, and they named him Hiyashi. Oshi died of cancer last year, and Ikano is raising the boys alone. It is my fervent prayer that some day he will find someone else to share his life. He deserves no less than the very best.

Watching our lives prosper, as did the country in those early post-war years, was a thrilling experience for all of us. The SENTINEL continued to grow as we moved into other avenues of communications with the purchase of radio station WXLI-108 in the spring of 1949. That fall, while visiting with my father at the mansion, he made note of a story we had featured earlier that week regarding the 83rd meeting of the Grand Army of the Republic, a group of surviving veterans of the Civil War. Six, of the sixteen still remaining, had made the encampment held in Indianapolis, Indiana. Dad had held the folded copy of the Sentinel on his lap and looked off into space for several moments, then turned to me and said, "My father fought in that war.": Three days later Dad died of a stroke. He was 75 years old.

In his will, Dan Reid Jr. had left particular instruction for his final rest. He was to be cremated and his ashes buried in a small isolated cemetery located somewhere in central Texas. His attorney ultimately explained this was, in fact, the burial site of my illustrious grandfather, Texas Ranger Daniel Reid Senior. Mother was in no condition to make such a trip and in the end, it was resolved that Jack and I, accompanied by his two sons Tom and Britt II, now 14 and 13 respectively. Ruth and Helen would stay with Mom and see to her needs while we were gone.

There are rare occasions in one's life when memories remain crystal clear throughout the years. That journey by train to Texas is as vivid today as though it were yesterday. Debarking in the small community of Redbud, a flea-bitten pock mark on the countryside, Jack, the boys and I rented several horses and some camping gear. Then we hired an old cowboy named Angus Potter to serve as our guide. The location of the grave site was inaccessible by road, being situated over a long winding ravine cut into the rugged hills called Brian's Gap. The two day horse trek was not quite the grand adventure my nephews had envisioned back in the comforts of home. By day we suffered dust and heat under a fierce sun while the nights were brutally cold. All of us would snuggle tightly in our bedrolls, crawling as close to the campfire as was safe. Only old potter, a grizzly faced, happy-go-lucky character seemed unaffected by the harshness of these surroundings. So in tuned with his environmet was he, it was easy to imagine his love for these parts as yet uncivilized open spaces.

At long last we reached Brian's Gap and the small plot of earth located on a high ridge above the ominous looking gulch. Bordered only by handset rocks, the unpretentious plot was identified by thirteen wooden crosses, most having fallen with time. Barely able to read the chiseled names on each plank, we silently set about returning the individual crosses to their proper stances and, in so doing, found the two which we had come so far to locate; Daniel Reid, Captain and John Reid, Trooper. In the spot between the two brothers, Jack and I dug a small hole and reverently set the urn with father's ashes into it. After burying the urn, Jack read a passage from Mother's Bible and then we simply stood there in silence. My mind was filled with images of my loving father and the many times he had regaled Jack and I with the fantastic story of John Reid and how he had miraculously escaped the massacre that had occurred in this place.

That evening, sitting around the blazing fire, not fifty yards from the ghosts of those brave men, Jack and I finally related the tale to young Tom and Britt II. Old Angus, wishing to respect our privacy, at what was clearly a family affair, had already laid out his roll by the horses and gone off to sleep. I watched the awe and disbelief in the boys' wide eyes. When those accounts were done, I then proceeded to shock them, including Jack, with the confession of my secret life as the notorious Green Hornet. It was a revelation that quickly prompted scores of questions from all three, and I spent most of the remainder of that eventful evening under the Texas stars doing my best to honestly answer each and every one of them. I'd like to believe it brought us closer together. It was a special night.

The next morning, we started for home and the continuation of our individual lives. Jack and Helen, soon after, made the decision to move to Florida. It was a booming area population wise and Jack began a highly successful architect career. After a few years establishing themselves in the sunny climate, they invited Mom to come live with them and after very little goading by Ruth and I, she accepted. Of course, we had to promise we would visit twice yearly and send her tons of pictures of Diana as she continued to blossom.

One of the big changes with Mom's decision was her stipulation that we move into the mansion, thus keeping it occupied. Even though my spacious apartment in the city was more adequate, the argument of raising Diana in the country was too strong to oppose. And if this is to be an honest recollection, I must also admit to delightfully relishing the thought of being the new Master Reid of the house. Thus, it was all done and we closed up most of the apartment except for a few rooms I still used whenever business kept me in town overnight.

Of course, no distance was ever too great to keep the Reids apart for too long, and both families visited back and forth on a regular basis. As the children matured, we naturally saw less and less of them. Even our own Diana, in her teen years, was seldom seen but for a whirling blur of pony tail and skirt as she chased from her upstairs room to a waiting car in the front yard filled with youthful peers. One of the genuine surprises during that period was the bond that developed between my namesake nephew Britt II and myself.

Choosing to attend City College and major in communications, Britt II happily surprised us all by requesting to stay with us during his school semesters. Ruth and I were quite fond of both Britt and his older brother, who attended Florida State as an Archeology major, but Britt II was special. Upon arriving that eventful fall Saturday morning, he seemed to fit almost immediately, as if the old structure had, in fact, been awaiting his presence. To Diana, he became a confidant and a big brother. We could not have been happier. Many are the nights he has joined me here, in this very library, staring up at the painting of our daring ancestor and then once more plaguing me, good-naturedly, on my own crime fighting years.

Last evening, I found him at my desk openly standing there, the right side drawer open. In his hands he held the green cloth that had so often hidden my face from deadly enemies. It was an odd sight, the crew-cut, clear eyed college boy holding up that icon to all we Reids had ever held dear. At last, he sensed my presence at the door, looked me straight in the eye and said with all the courage his voice could muster, "Uncle Britt, someday I want to be the Green Hornet."

Tonight, as those words echo in my heart, I am both excited and scared. Is he serious? Can he possibly know what he is getting himself into? Of course not. Yet why do I feel there is a good chance that boy will make it happen? I must contact Ikano as soon as possible. He will know how best to advise me.

A new Green Hornet? It boggles the mind. Then again, why not? Why not indeed!

BRITT REID
15 MAY 1955

THE REID FAMILY TREE

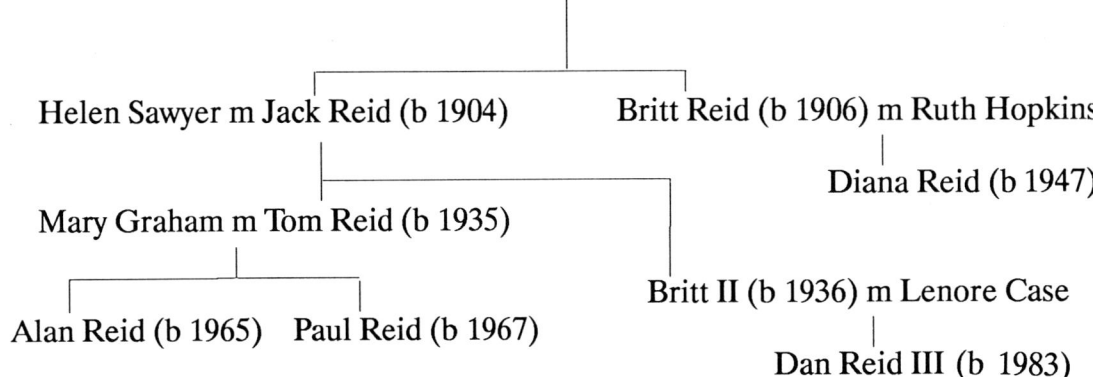

THE KATO FAMILY TREE

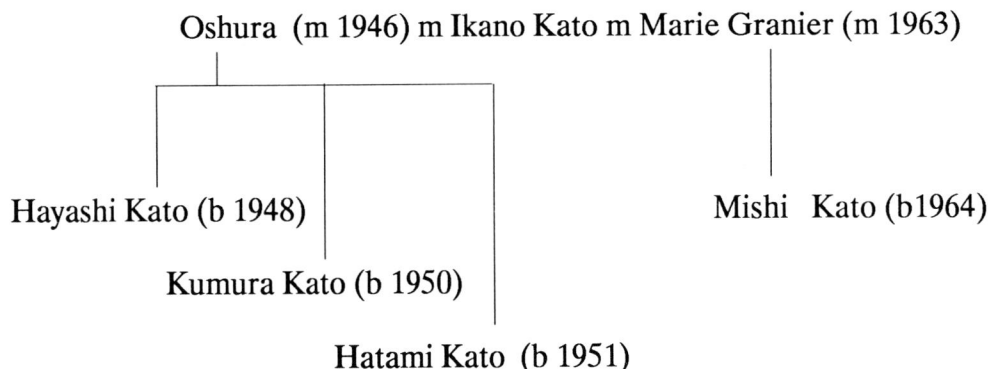

MY LAST CASE—CONTINUED

Ron Fortier — Writer
Jeff Butler — Penciler
David Mowry — Inker
The Now Staff — Colorists
Dan Nakrosis & Patrick Williams — Letterers
Michele Mach — Art Director
Katherine Llewellyn — Editor
Tony Caputo — Editor-in-Chief

CAN THE CLIPPINGS IN A SCRAPBOOK UNRAVEL THE SECRETS OF THE PAST?

EACH GRINNING FACE BECOMES A PIECE IN THE PUZZLE.

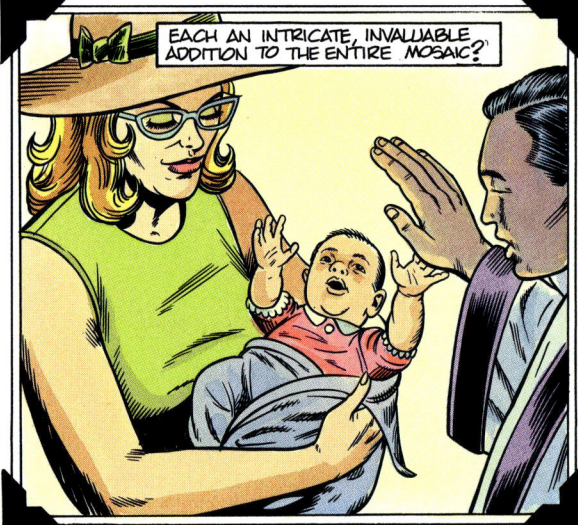

EACH AN INTRICATE, INVALUABLE ADDITION TO THE ENTIRE MOSAIC?

WHAT IS THE PRICE OF THIS CANVAS?

IS IT HAPPINESS AND DREAMS FULFILLED?

LEGEND

Daily Sentinel

15¢ | WEATHER COOL AND OVERCAST HIGH 56, LOW 33

EARLY EDITION — OCTOBER 3, 1979

MOB BOSS GUNNED DOWN

GREEN HORNET PRIME SUSPECT IN DEVANE MURDER. VICTIM'S SON VOWS REVENGE

Late last night, the notorious known criminal allegedly added murder to his list of deeds. Retired mob figure, Joey "Jackknife" Devane was shot to death with a .38 caliber police special. According to David Devane, the victim's son and the sole witness to the shooting, the Hornet entered the Brentwood residence shortly after midnight accompanied by an accomplice.

COMMUNICATIONS MAGNATE SUFFERS CORONARY

Millionaire playboy, and General Manager of the Reid Communications Network, Britt Reid II, suffered a heart attack and was rushed to Mount Mercy hospital in the early hours of the morning.

Present at his bedside were Britt and Ruth Reid, former publishers of the DAILY SENTINEL, and Reid's two nephews, Alan and Paul. Hospital officials say Reid's condition is guarded, but doctor's are optimistic.

TO BE CONTINUED

OBITUARIES

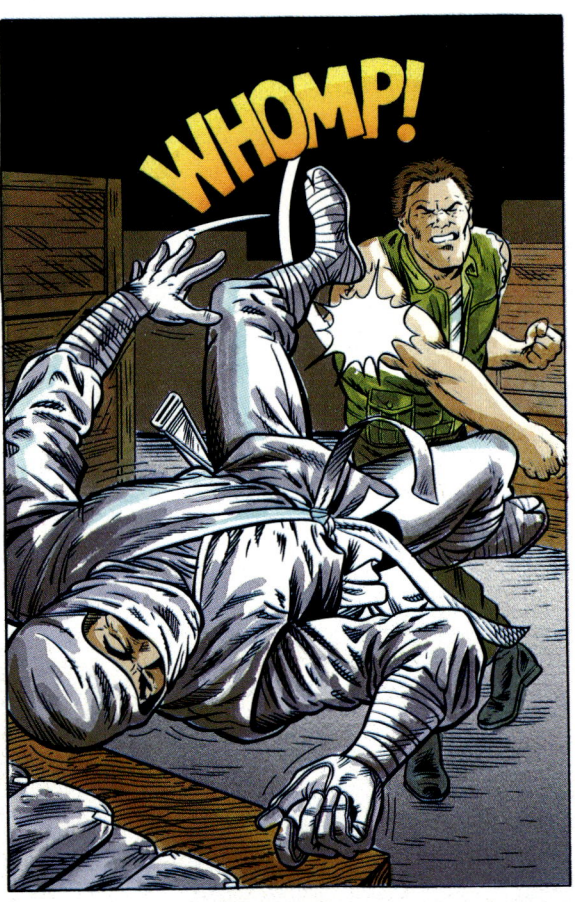

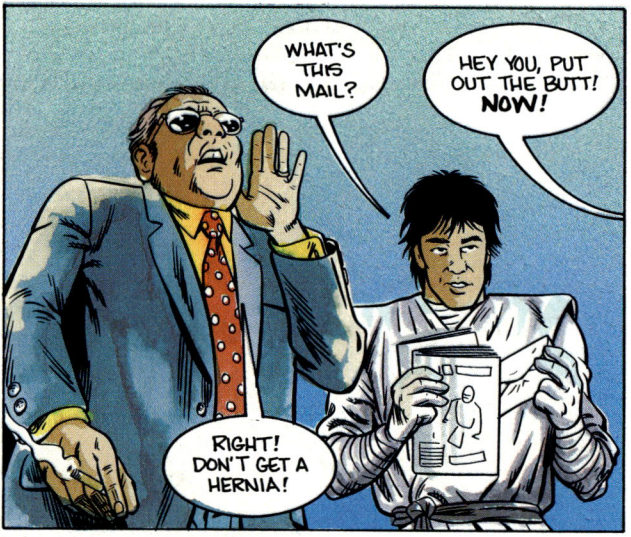

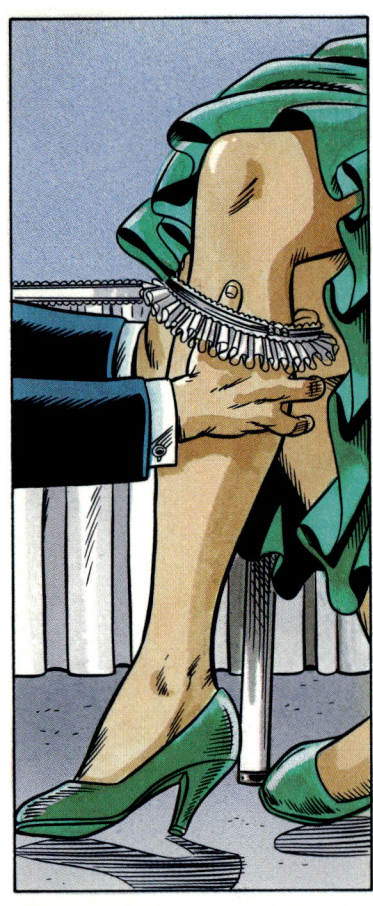

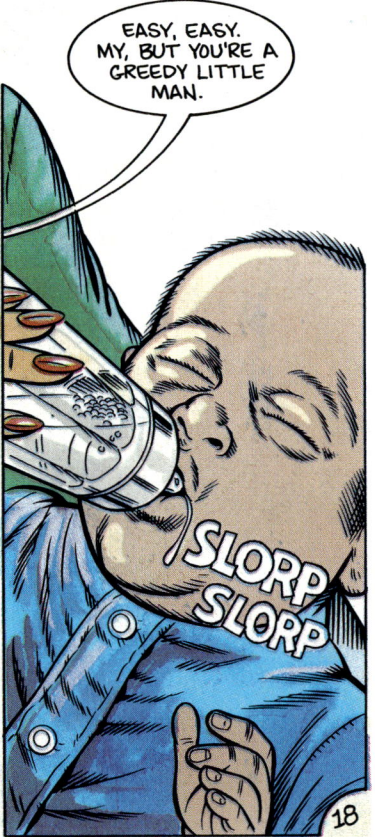

REQUIEM AND REBIRTH

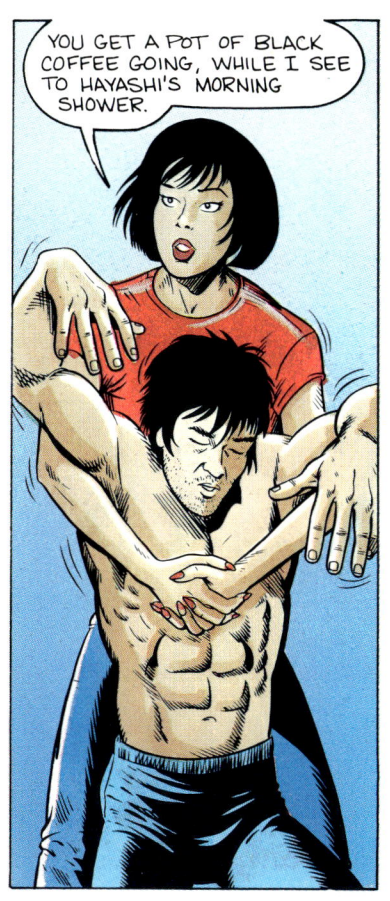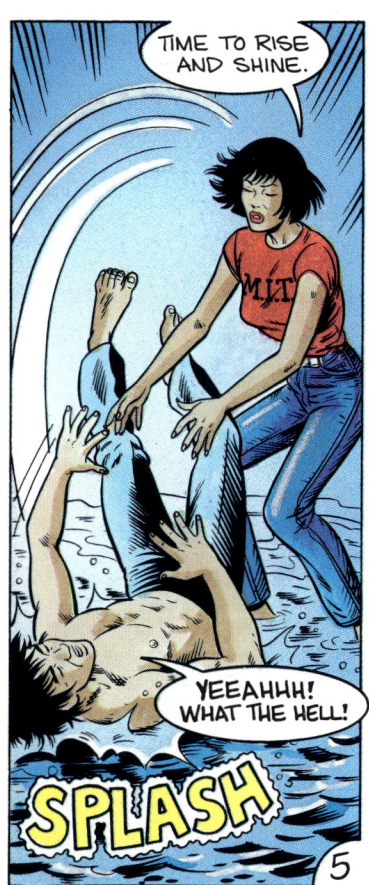

THE NEW GREEN HORNET

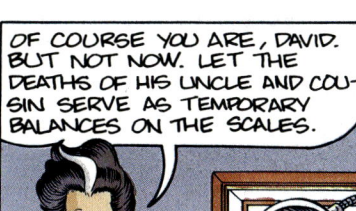

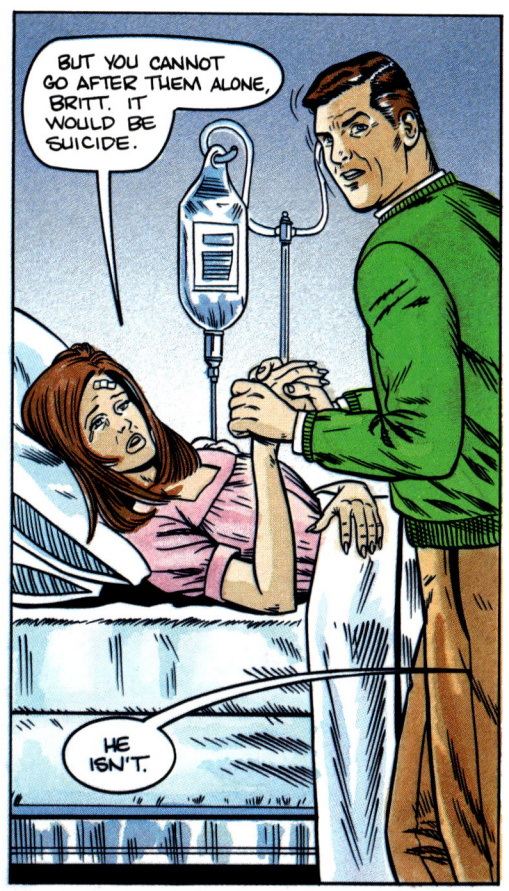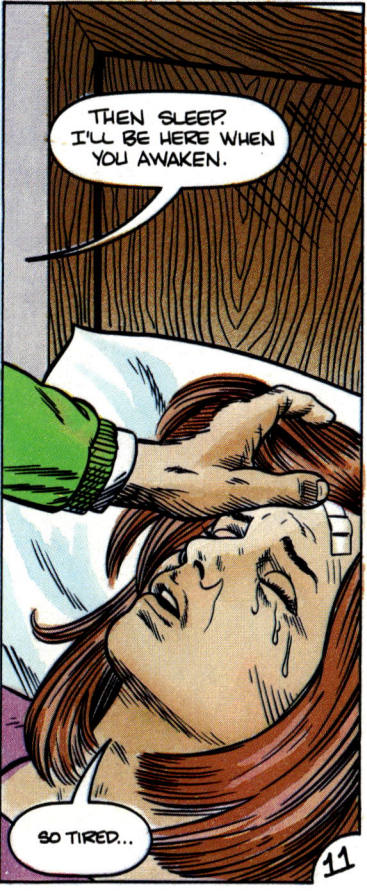

BLOODLINES

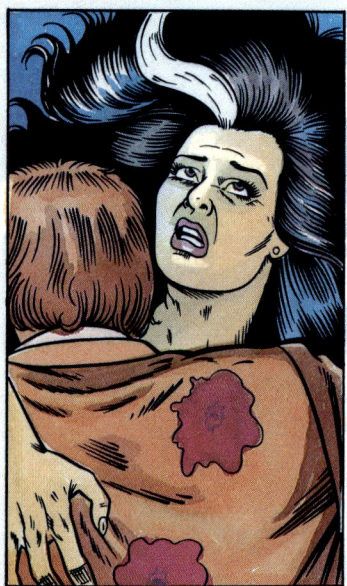

ON THE PAD

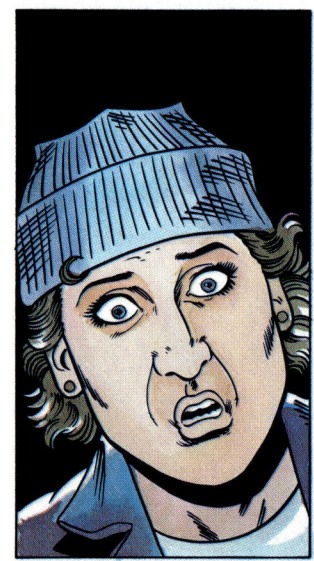

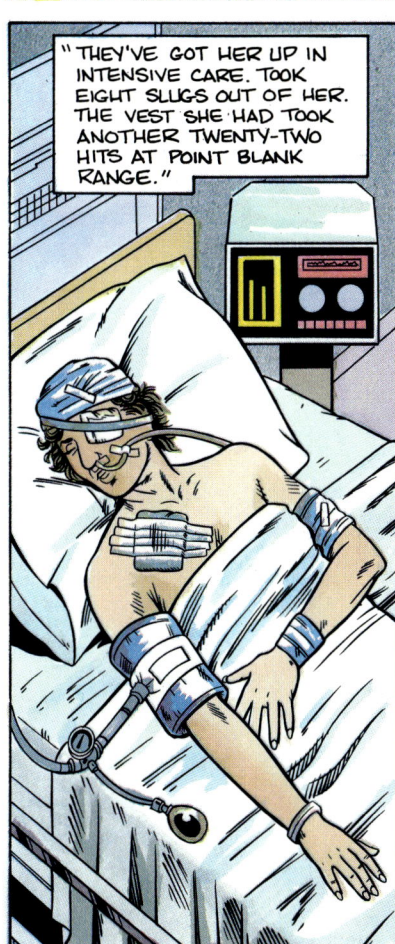

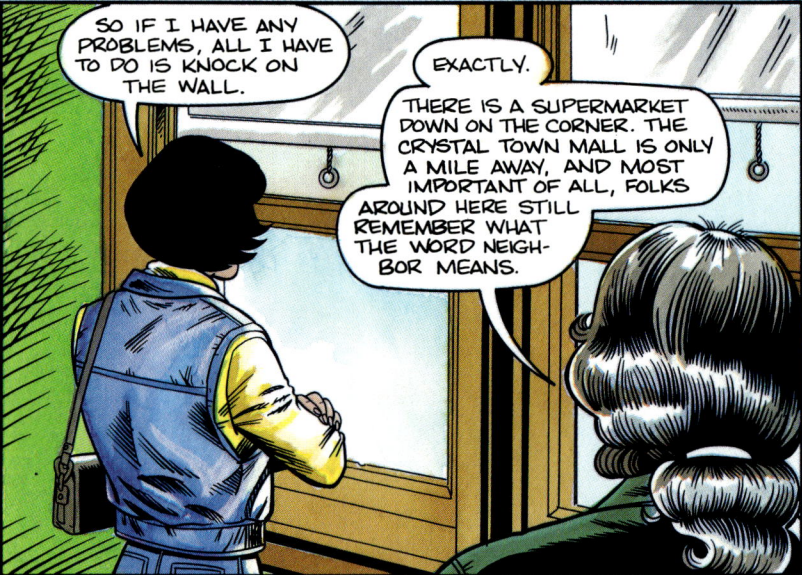

ON THE PAD—PART TWO

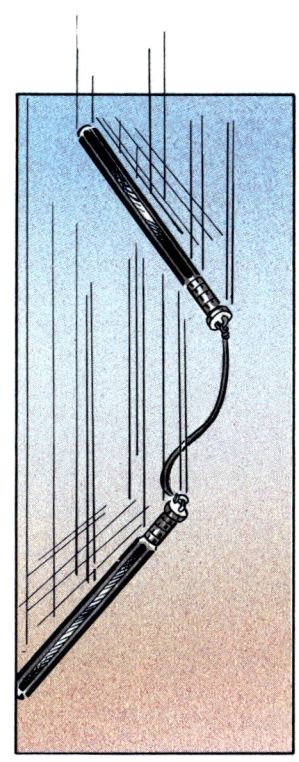

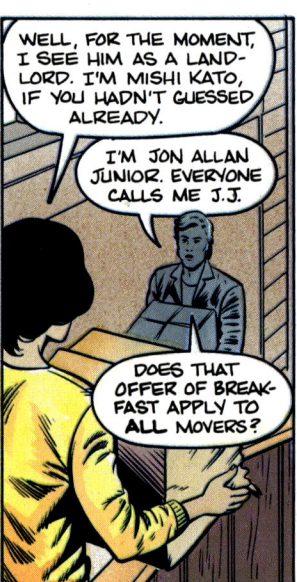

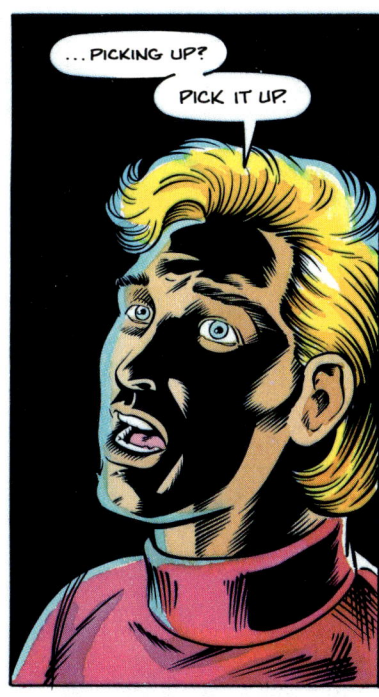

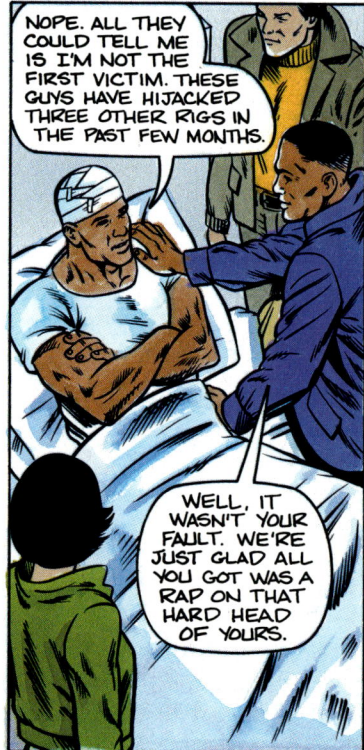

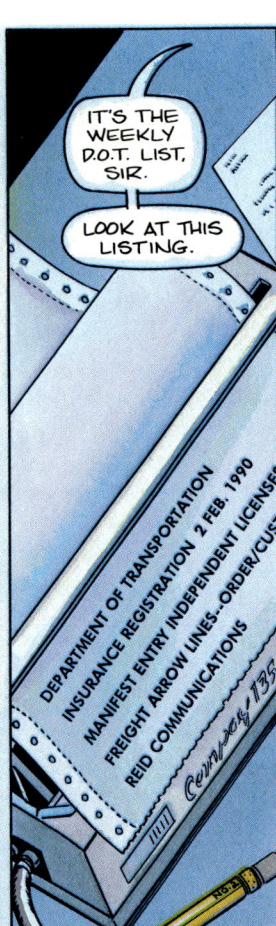

A MEMORY OF DEATH

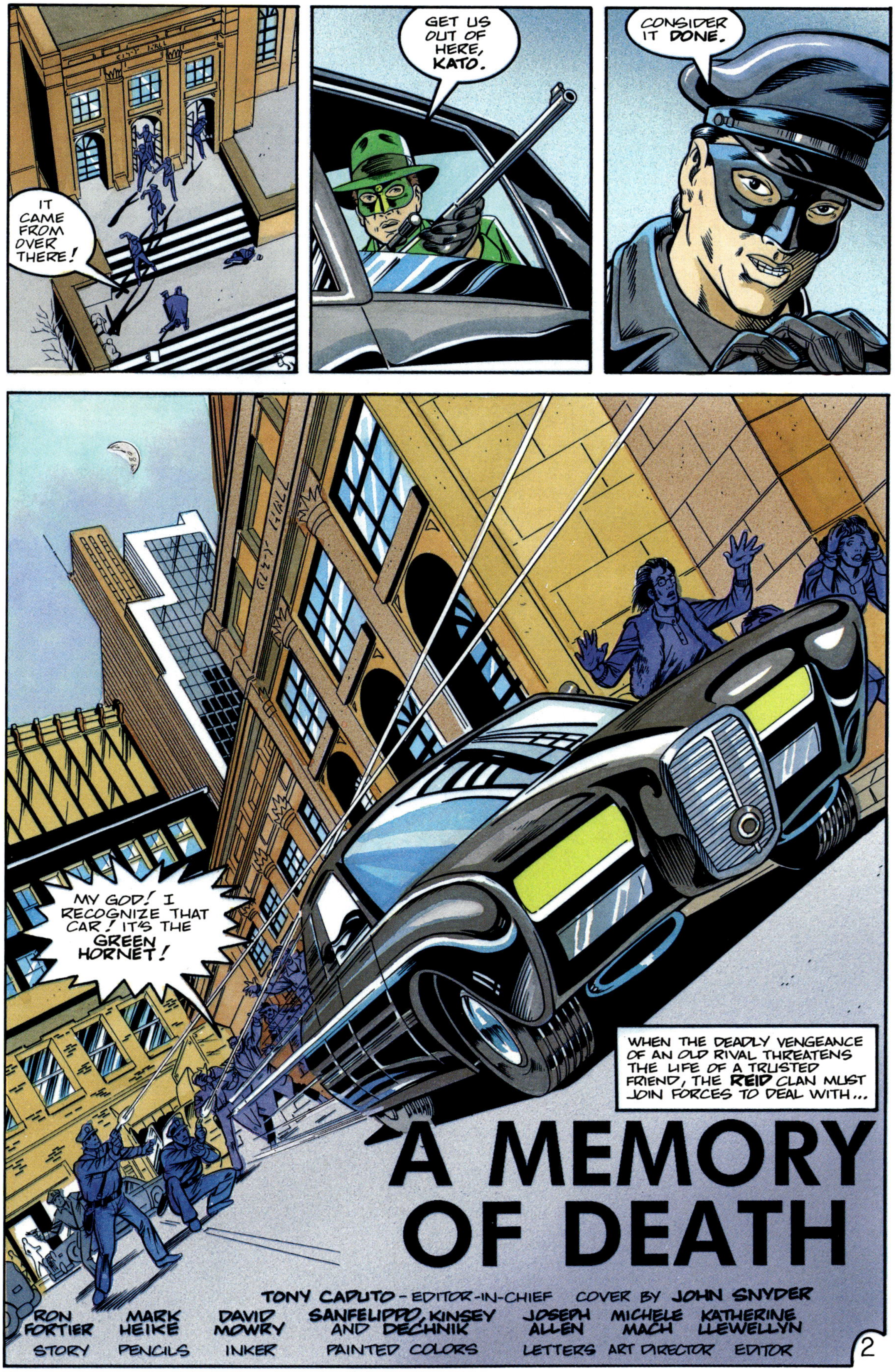

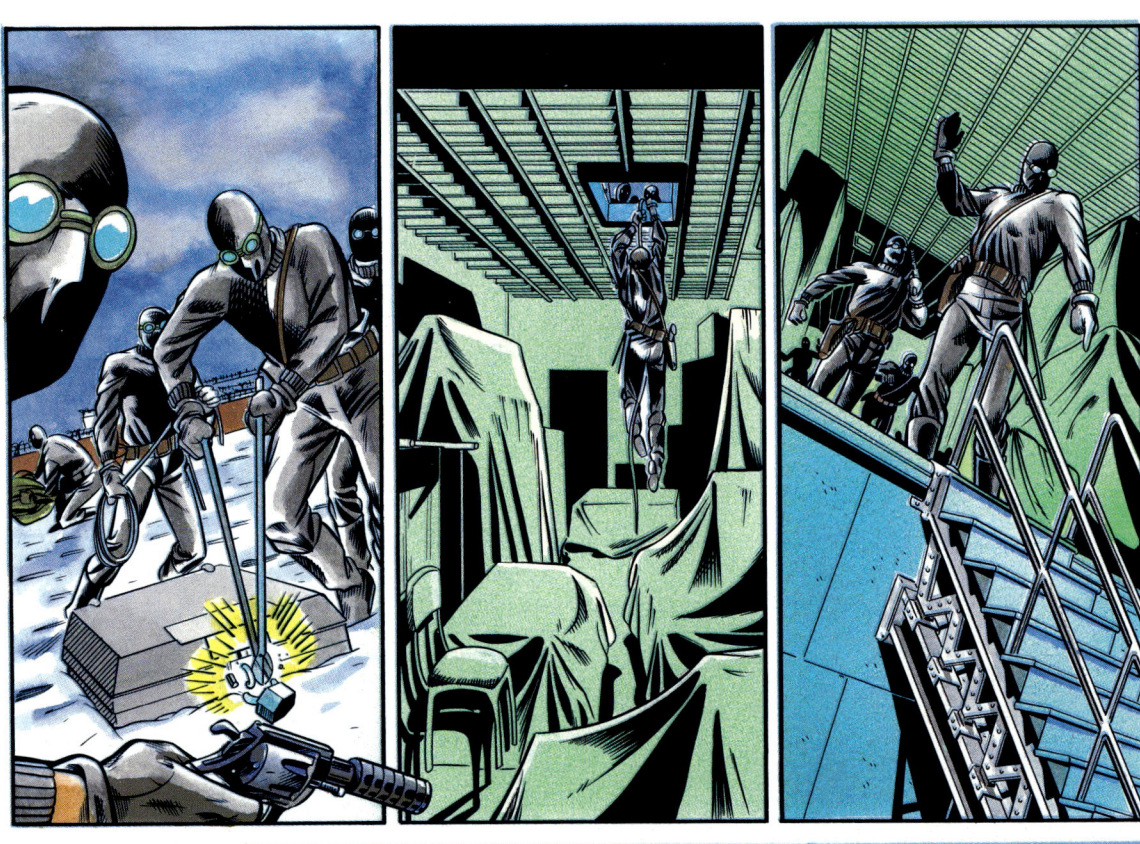

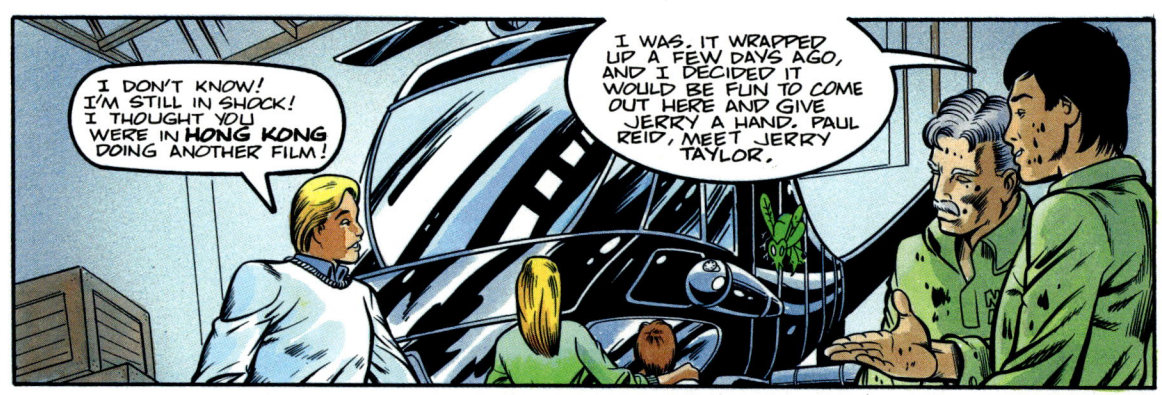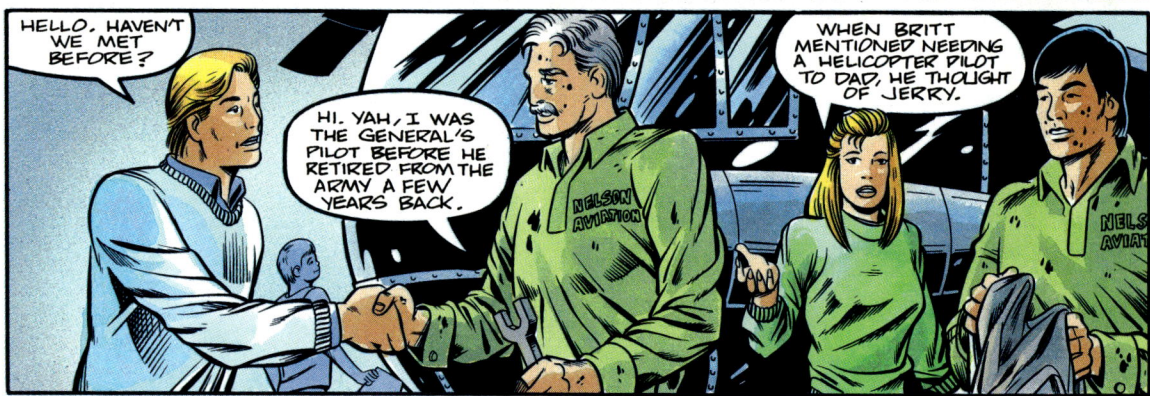

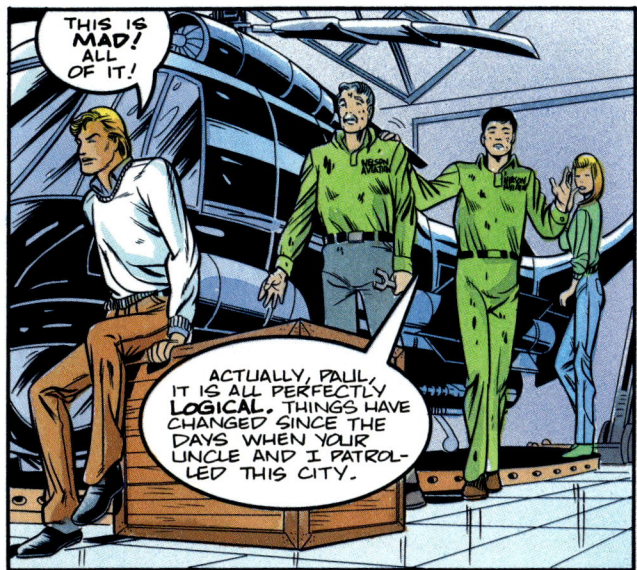

SUNSET OVER THE WHITE MOUNTAINS OF NEW HAMPSHIRE...

FOR SOME IT IS A SLICE OF PARADISE ON EARTH..

FORMER DA FRANK SCANLON FINDS IT A SETTING FOR PERSONAL TERROR.

"THIS IS CRAZY, MITCHELL! WHAT DO YOU HOPE TO GAIN BY ANY OF THIS?"

"A LITTLE PAYBACK, MR. SCANLON. NINETEEN YEARS WORTH, AS I FIGURE IT."

A MEMORY OF DEATH PART 2

DOUG TALLALA COVER ART

RON FORTIER • TOD SMITH • DAVID MOWRY • HOLLY SANFELIPPO • J. ALLEN
STORY PENCILS INKS KELLY KINSEY LETTERS
           SUZANNE DECHNIK
MICHELE MACH • KATY LLEWELLYN • TONY CAPUTO PAINTED COLORS
ART DIRECTOR EDITOR EDITOR-IN-CHIEF

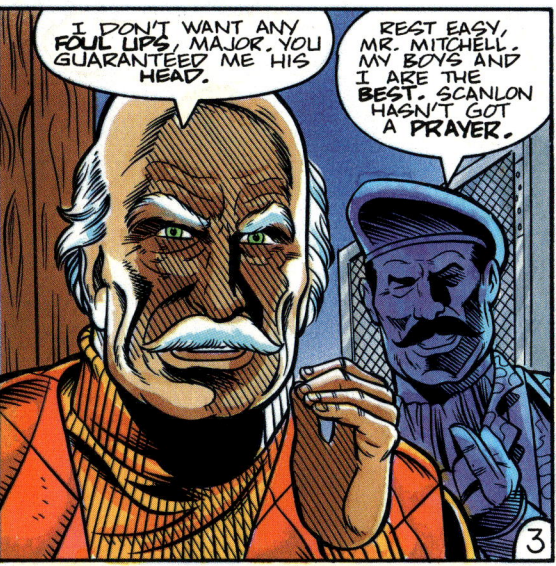

FAR FROM THE HILLS OF NEW HAMPSHIRE ON THE TOP FLOOR OF THE REID TOWER...

ALL SYSTEMS ON THE **BLACK STINGER** ARE GO. LET'S MOVE IT, PEOPLE!

DON'T WORRY, BRITT. WE'LL FIND **FRANK** AND BRING HIM HOME.

IT SEEMS LIKE YOU'RE ALWAYS HERE WHEN THE CHIPS ARE DOWN, HAYASHI. KEEP AN EYE ON THE KID.

GOSH, I WISH I COULD GO!

MAYBE **NEXT** TIME, BUCKAROO. RIGHT NOW YOU CAN HELP YOUR DAD WITH THE ROOF CONTROLS!

YOU BET! COME ON, DAD!

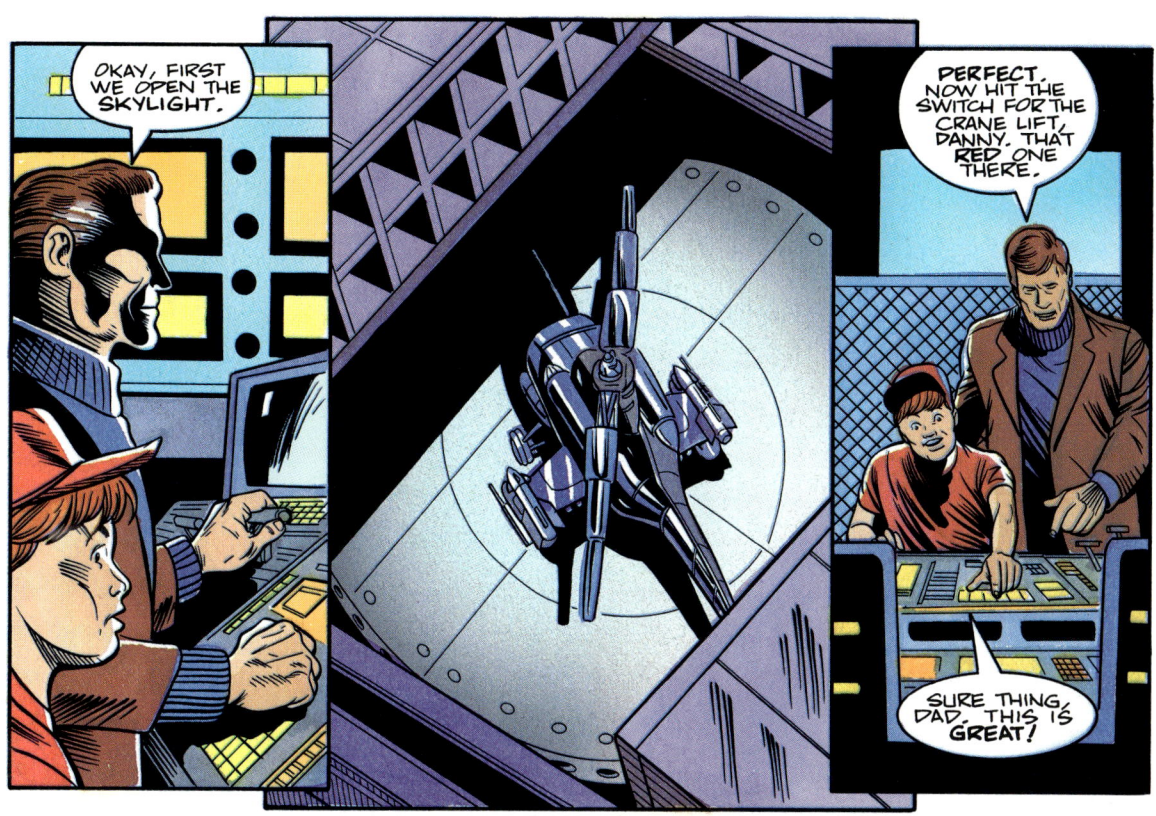

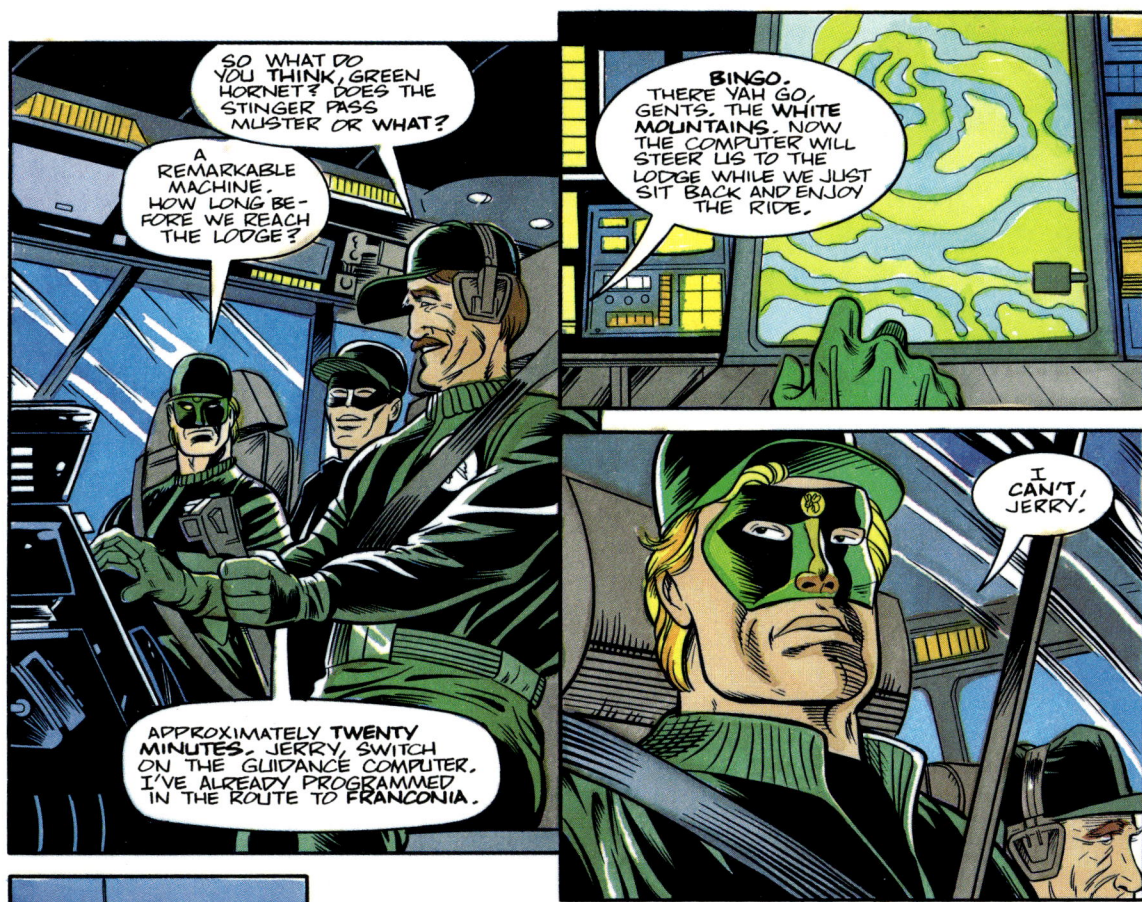

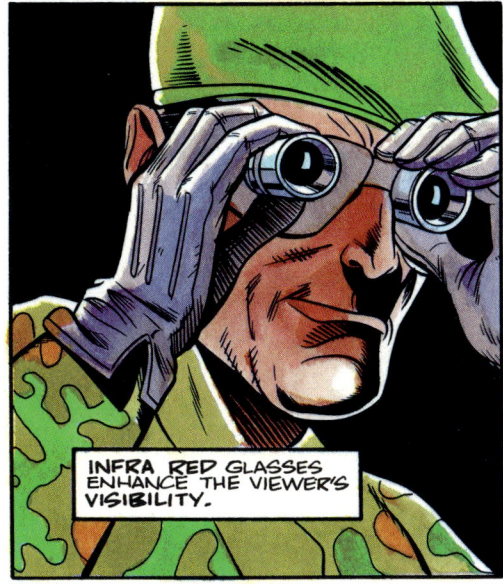

A MEMORY OF DEATH— PART TWO